T0197476

BOOTS
THE
BUNNY BEAGLE

Marcy L. Bowser

Illustrated by: Dawn McPeek-Bowser
Edited by: Julie Spaulding

To order additional copies of this book, contact:
Xlibris
844-714-8691
www.Xlibris.com
Orders@Xlibris.com

ISBN: Softcover   978-1-6698-2339-1
       EBook   978-1-6698-2340-7

Print information available on the last page

Rev. date: 05/03/2022

There once was a man named Homer who owned a puppy kennel, at his kennels he bred and raised many different kinds of puppies. He had German Shepherds, Collies, and other breeds; but his pride and joy were his Beagles.

He raised Show Beagles and Hunting Beagles and his Beagles were the best beagles to be found anywhere.

1

One day a new litter of puppies (Beagles) were born to Homer's prize Beagle, Millicent; Millicent was always proud of her puppies. Homer went to look at the new puppies, when he noticed a little runt puppy pushed to the back of the box. The other pups were all feeding but this little pup was so tiny he had been pushed out of the way by his bigger brothers and sisters. Homer picked up the little runt and took a good look at him. He could tell he had displaced hips, he knew then this little guy could never be a Show Beagle or a Hunting Beagle.

In Homer's mind this little beagle would never be good for anything so he placed the little pup in his big pocket until he decided what to do with him.

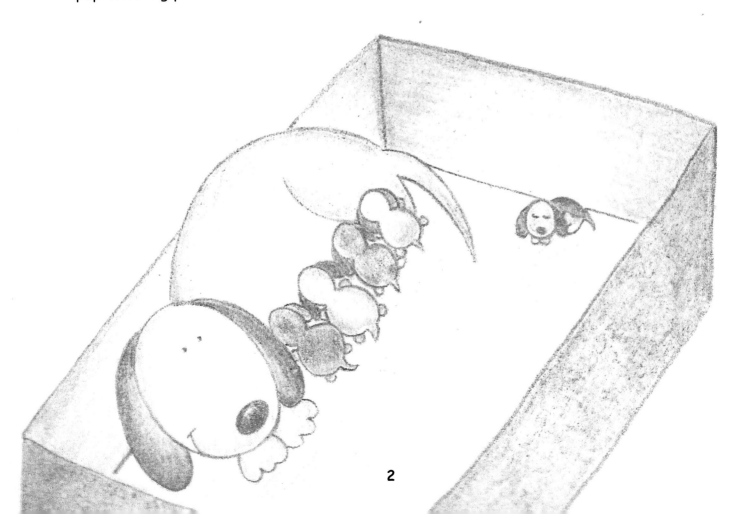

Millicent the mommy beagle was very upset when she seen her smallest pup was gone.
Although she had other pups to feed and raise; it broke her heart that one was gone.

Homer took the little pup to his helper Nathan and asked him to get rid of the pup. He did not want this puppy at his kennel, because of his size and the disabilities that would be caused by his displaced hips.

Nathan really liked the little puppy even though he didn't have his eyes open yet, he wanted to keep the pup but knew he might lose his job if he did. Nathan was very young and he and his wife were struggling to get by; most of his friends were in the same boat. Nathan didn't know anyone who could take the pup and he didn't have the money to take him to the local animal shelter.

Nathan's wife asked him to stop at the store to pick up some groceries on his way home that night; he had placed the tiny pup in his big coat pocket. Nathan stopped at the grocery, next to the grocery was a pet store, in front of the pet store there were some cages with different pets. There was a hamster cage, a guinea pig cage, and a rabbit cage with a new mommy rabbit and her little ones. Many people were stopping and looking at the animals.

Nathan sauntered over to look at the animals as he truly loved animals and was upset as to what to do with this little pup in his pocket. As he was standing looking at the bunny cage he seen what a good mother the mama Bunny was, on impulse he slipped the little beagle pup out of his pocket and put him in the Bunny cage back in a shadow where he wasn't so noticeable. As he walked off he said a prayer that the mama bunny would take good care of the pup.

The little pup, his eyes opening for the first time seen this animal with big tall ears and a white tail, he heard such a sweet voice, but she was looking at him with great big eyes full of surprise and wonder. Ms. Bunny as all of her children called her, had always lived in the cage in the pet store, and she didn't know who this little guy was, she could see he was a baby, but he was much bigger than her babies, but a baby nevertheless. She could also see that this was a hungry baby, but he wasn't strong like her babies, and he wasn't moving his little back legs. He was just laying there looking at her with eyes full of love and joy because he thought she was his mommy.

Ms. Bunny having a mother's heart could see this little guy needed her; she did not have the heart to turn her back on him. She looked at the pup and decided to call him Boots because all his feet were white like he was wearing little boots. She knew in her Bunny heart that he would never survive if he didn't use those little back legs. She looked at him and said "Sweetie I'm going to name you Boots, but if you want to eat you'll have to come over here on your own, I have plenty of milk for all of my children."

Little Boots struggled over to join the other babies for dinner; Ms. Bunny introduced him to her family as Boots their new baby brother. The little baby bunnies were delighted to have him there, and welcomed him into the family.

Boots thrived with the Bunnies, and he loved his new found family but he loved Ms. Bunny the most. Even though Boots couldn't hop like his brothers and sisters, but kind of scooted around, they adored him too. He was very happy.

Everyday Boots was becoming stronger; much to the satisfaction of Ms. Bunny he was using his back legs more and more. Boots loved his bunny brothers and sisters, but most of all he loved Ms. Bunny who fed him and made sure he was warm. Every night he would snuggle between his bunny brothers and sisters to keep warm. He was a happy puppy.

Alas Boots was fast outgrowing his bunny brother and sisters; and this made him very noticeable. The Pet Store owner Hal was cleaning the bunny cage when he noticed Boots - He definitely was not a Bunny! Dismayed he had to figure out what to do with this pup!

He couldn't sell the puppy as he wasn't sure what kind of pup he was or if he was a mixed breed. Hal decide to call some friends and offer the pup free to whoever wanted him.

Ms. Bunny and her family were very much dismayed and heartbroken when Boots was taken out of the Bunny cage – but sadly she learned to accept that soon all her little bunnies would be gone to new homes. Boots was heartbroken too; this was the only family he had ever known.

A young friend of his took the pup as he was in college he couldn't keep the pup, but called his dad and his dad agreed to take Boots. Mr. John took the pup home to his wife who immediately threw her arms up in dismay! A puppy so hard to take care of and we already have a dog! But having a mother's heart she soon seen this little guy needed a home and love (as Ms. Bunny had) he soon became her baby as all her children had grown-up and left home.

Boots loved his new family and they loved him. John and Lynette named him Boots because of his four white paws which made him look like he was wearing boots. The other dog was a rescue dog from a farm. His name was Big Brown, because he was a big brown dog; he was very wise and also very protective of Boots. When Big Brown lived on the farm, he always watched over all the pups born there, and kept them out of the woods so they wouldn't get lost.

Boots new family had a nice backyard, he and Big Brown would lie out there for hours sunning themselves, and sometimes they would play a game. Big Brown enjoyed Boots company very much; they soon became best buddies. Boots looked up to Big Brown; he had his rules - always protect your family and your home. Big Brown lived for when his people petted him and praised him; they loved him very much, and knew he was a very wise dog.

John and Lynette also had three granddaughters, these three little girls were very mischievous, plus they all three talked a lot, they loved 8ig Brown and Boots, and Big Brown and Boots adored them. Strange thing no one noticed that Boots had a bad limp and that Big Brown was old, they just loved them for what they were, kind gentle dogs.

Boots himself was a very kind sweet loving dog; who wouldn't hurt anyone especially a rabbit.

Boots and Big Brown were in the backyard one day, when a bunny hopped out. Boots went running over so happy to see a relative, he called out "Bunny, hello..." the bunny looked at him with big eyes than quickly hopped away. Boots was so disappointed and hung his head down. "What's wrong?" asked Big Brown. Boots replied "I bet that was a relative of mine and instead of saying hello they hopped away. What's wrong with me?" Big Brown looked at Boots quizzically and said "Do you think you're a bunny?" Boots said "Oh yes that bunny looked just like my brothers and sisters at the pet store, before I came here. Big Brown was really confused then he said "You're not a bunny you're a dog, actually you're a beagle." Boots said in amazement "I'm a dog! A beagle!" Big Brown nodded yes. Boots stammered "but beagles hunt bunnies I would never do that! My mommy was a bunny and so were my brothers and sisters!"

Big Brown could see he had a very confused Beagle on his paws. He explained to Boots all about how Beagles are used to hunt rabbits and how they are natural enemies. Boots was broken-hearted he could never hurt a rabbit, he thought about his mommy Ms. Bunny and how she would comfort him when he felt awkward or different, and how she had helped him overcome his disability. Big Brown took Boots in front of a mirror, when Boots seen his reflection he started barking, then he realized he really was a dog, a beagle at that. Big Brown comforted Boots and told him that being a beagle was a good thing and that no one cared that he didn't get around quite as well as most beagles. Big Brown told Boots "Just be your natural Bunny Beagle self."

It took a while for Boots too adjust to the idea he was actually a Beagle, but it became much easier with the love of the three granddaughters; Marie, Dawn and Mae. They always wanted to pet him and hold him. He and Big Brown were their buddies whenever they stayed with Grandma and Papaw.

It also helped Boots when the bunnies in the yard accepted him, when they found out he had been raised by Ms. Bunny, well that made him family.

As little Mae said "I love Boots and he loves me" Boots nodded thinking "yes he couldn't change, but no one here expected him too, they loved him just the way he was."

This is how two "throw-away" dogs became best friends, and were able to accept themselves and each other as they were; because after all who could throw away all that love.

Printed in the United States
by Baker & Taylor Publisher Services